For all who suffered war and violence

Silent Night
Holy Night

*Memories of the last Christmas Eve
during World War II*

carried together and written down by

Antonia Katharina Tessnow

TWENTYSIX – Der Self-Publishing-Verlag
Eine Kooperation zwischen der Verlagsgruppe Random
House und BoD – Books on Demand

© 2017 Antonia Katharina Tessnow

Herstellung und Verlag:
BoD – Books on Demand, Norderstedt

ISBN: **9783740733179**

Übersetzung: **Antonia Katharina Tessnow**

From the diary of my mothers sister
Berlin 1944

We lived in Berlin Mahlsdorf, while in spring of 1943 the bomb attacks of the city increased to such a massive intent, that they reached the suburbs. They've just started to build a big bunker in our neighborhood, ever since more and more families got buried alive in the basements of their houses. This is why my father decided to send us children to the countryside, where it was relatively safe.

Ketzin is a small, quiet village, surrounded by the most beautiful fields and woods. The landscape looked like fairyland to us. One of my fathers friends, a war veteran from world war I, owned a farm. There we were welcomed by his family and stayed for several months. Our mother and we two little girls were sent here to recover from horrors and the fright of the bomb-war.

Ketzin is only 150 Miles away from Berlin, but we didn't notice anything of the daily bomb attacks of the cities. In the beginning I mistrusted the quietness. I was so full of tension that I was ready to snap off and jump to find safety and protection at any given time. It took a few days until I build enough confidence to play with the other kids on the farm without fear. But just when I have almost forgotten the war, a siren went on. My sister and I jumped immediately and ran. Our eyes searched the sky. There were still no bombers in sight, so we rushed into the house to grab our few belongings.

Just when we ran in the direction of the cellar storeroom, the sirens went silent. What we heard was guffawing laughter instead. The other kids were laughing at *us*. When they told us, that it was just the fire department performing their monthly test alarm, we had to laugh in relief, too.

All of a sudden, the war was nothing but a fading memory of an almost forgotten life. We learned again to sleep through the night and to sleep into the mornings. We learned how to deal with animals and helped in the fields. I went to the small village school and in the mornings, after we got up, we got fresh milk to drink, that the father brought directly from the stables and which was still warm. This is how a wonderful summer and a peaceful autumn passed by. It was almost heavenly.

Meanwhile the construction of the concrete-bunker made such progress that we could return to Berlin and when the air raid warnings started, we could flee into the bunker.

On November 18, 1943, loaded with suitcases and baskets, just as we arrived in our old apartment, the sirens came on. Hastily we grabbed our luggage and seeked shelter in the bunker. Even though the first bombs hit the ground, we didn't even think about leaving a single case behind. They were stuffed with sausages and bacon from Ketzin, priceless treasures, which were scarce goods in the war-torn city.

The boom of the explosions seem to give us wings and this is how we made it to the new bunker, safe and sound, without a single scratch. But our souls got hit and were deeply wounded. The relaxation of the last months completely vanished within this very moment. In the morning of the same day we still felt the sunshine on our faces and had the fresh air from the countryside in our lungs, and now we sat, surrounded by walls several meters thick, on the cold, wet floor and tasted the dust of destroyed concrete. We completely ran out of breath. How goodly it was in the small village!

Now there were attacks almost every evening, sometimes even in the middle of the night. When we left the bunker, the entire city was buried under a huge, red-glowing fire flash. We've been black from soot that covered everything, every time. Our hand baggage, including a blanket and a gas mask, has always been ready and it just took us seconds to get dressed as soon as the sirens went on.

"Is the bunker really bomb proof?", that has often been our anxious question to our father.

It was, as we should see while the war continued and the bombings got worse and worse.

Christmas was getting closer. Everything was cleaned up and the big Christmas tree was already well-placed in the living room. Grandma and Aunt Frieda spend the night at our house. We wanted to celebrate Christmas together. The bunker was nearby, which made us all sleep better and allowed us to await the holidays a bit more relaxed.

At an unusual time - at seven o'clock in the morning - on December 24th, the sirens went on. While we jumped out of bed and rushed in our clothes, we already heard the deep buzzing of the airplanes, that became louder and louder and as we stepped out of the house, it looked like the entire city was illuminated like brought daylight. The flak fired without respite. A frightening noise.

Mommy, Grandma, Aunt Frieda and I ran in panic in the direction of the bunker. My sister and Family Gruber ran with Daddy in the basement, because they didn't dare to hush outside. But the basement was hardly safe.

My sister later wrote in her diary: 'When it occurred to get a little quieter, my father hasted together with me to the bunker. Around us it flashed and crashed, only above us it didn't. I just thought: *When we would only already be there!* When we reached the bunker I jumped from the bicycle. Daddy wanted to turn around, but all of a sudden there fell bombs very close by. I was looking for Mom and my sister down in the bunker, but I couldn't find them. Now I got scared.'

But how have others we been, when we ran away during the heavy attacks? We hustled down the street, together with a few others, up to the corner where we should have turned. Here grocer Kolbe stood in front of his house and directed us into the earth-bunker in his backyard. It crashed and fired above us. We stood tightly serried together, cheek-by-jowl in this narrow earth hole. The walls were shaking with every explosion. Earth rippled down and there was constant crying and screaming around us.

I was sitting on my small suitcase, held my ears and smiled at Grandma, Mom and Aunt Frieda. Later they told me how brave I have been and that I gave them confidence. But I was also very afraid. I probably just hid it behind the smile that covered

my face like a mask when the bombs hit the ground.
Suddenly it became more and more quiet. The sounds of the bombers got distant and ebbed away. Silence. We listened expectantly. Then we finally heard the clearing signal.
We climbed out of our earth hole. The rows of houses thinned out. Entire apartment buildings got destroyed and were now nothing but debris and dust. Sometimes there was just one wall missing, so we could easily look right into the rooms. In a few cases, the entire furniture was still standing there.
My heart started racing just before we turned around the corner.
What if our house got hit? I thought about Daddy and my sister who searched shelter in the basement. When a bomb has hit our house directly from above, they wouldn't have had the slightest chance to survive. I closed my eyes.

"They are alive!" I heard my mother screaming.

Our house was still standing. Daddy and my sister were waiting in front and waved at us. This is how we came back together in the end, relieved and unharmed.
But how did our apartment look like, that we just cleaned up and finished?
Every single window was broken; the darkening roller blinds hang in shreds, the plaster has fallen down and covered everything. The Christmas tree fell down and looked all grey now.

'Fortunately it wasn't decorated yet', we kept saying to ourselves.

At our neighbors, Family Grubers apartment, the tree has already been decorated and has fallen with the entire decoration and the beautiful musical clock, which we all used to love so much. That did look sad!

Many things have been torn apart and got destroyed. But the excitement about the holy night awoke inside of us despite all horrors.

We swept and wiped and dusted and cleaned; everything was supposed to look festive. Here and there, fear took over and we wondered if we could live through the night without bomb attacks? We just hoped for it.

After all the work, we tried to find some sleep. But none of us could really manage, after all the turmoil we've been through.

When the sun had set and it slowly got dark outside, the long awaited moment finally had come. The ball rang-in the holy night. The scent of the Christmas tree drew through all rooms and it looked glorious and beautiful.

We children spoke our poems and the exchange of presents followed, which we've awaited with great excitement. We've already been in the 5th year of war, so it was very unspectacular. But the joy overweighted everything.

Then we went to see Family Gruber in their apartment. The mother played the piano and like every year we sang 'Silent Night, Holy Night'.

Their tree also gleamed again. The nice, old musical clock was standing under the tree and turned around itself in front of our admiring eyes.

The spirit of the holy night was sensible in the entire house. We just realized that we were allowed to spend a peaceful evening. No sirens; no bombs; no bunkers. Our hope has come true.

That night we all stayed together for a long time and enjoyed this wonderful Christmas atmosphere. Nobody knew how long it would last. And we also knew, that a lot of our fellow people have lost everything today: All their belongings; children their toys; others the roof over their heads or even their lives. Many people were injured, buried alive, or have lost their loved ones. We, on the other hand, were full of gratitude to have gotten away with just a shock.

One more time we had to live through Christmas during war times, until we could finally celebrate this wonderful holiday in peace. A privilege given to us up to this very day.

From the diary of my mothers sister
Berlin 1944

Antonia Katharina Tessnow
Mecklenburg-Vorpommern, Germany 2017

Antonia Katharina Tessnow, Germany 2016

About the Author:

Antonia Katharina Tessnow was born in November 15, 1975 in Berlin. After finishing the evangelic school of Steglitz in Germany she graduated from High School in Iowa, United States. After her one year of student exchange she returned to Germany and worked many years professionally as a horse-back-trainer. At the age of 22 she moved to the north of Germany, worked in a sports stable and specialized in dressage. There she trained and qualified horses in all level of performances.

In the age of 28 she returned to her hometown and worked in the Olympic Stadion where she worked 6 years for the national association of modern pentathlon and trained athletes in the discipline of show jumping. Extra occupational she studied holistic medicine, holistic veterinary science and holistic psychology. Furthermore she passed a three year advanced educational class on the Institute of Emotional Processing.

In her mid-30th, after finishing all her educations, she left equestrianism to take advanced educational courses at the Devi Clinic in Sri Lanka and acquired her international authorization to work holistically in medicine. In the following three years she commuted between the United States and India to lead psycho-energetic healing sessions.

Antonia Katharina Tessnow is Doctor of holistic Medicine and Psychology, gained a wide spread comprehension of alternative healing methods, including the therapeutical use of music. She visited classes of one of the leading reincarnation therapists today, Trutz Hardo. During her stay in India she specialized in psycho-energetic and musical healing work, reincarnation therapy and phytomedicine.

Since 2009 she returned to Germany and dedicates her life not only to her artistical, holistic medical and authorical work but also her new found love and passion: The luxury Russian dog breed called Bolonka Zwetna.

Besides her holistic work of all kinds, which she further intensified, she trained as a groomer and completed additional education in keeping, breeding and animal lore. Today she lives close to a small village in Mecklenburg-Vorpommern, authors books and leads the professional dog breeding station called the 'Zarenhunde aus dem Alten Jagdhaus'.

Website of the Author:

www.antonia-katharina.de

Website of the Kennel 'aus dem Alten Jagdhaus':

rund-um-hunde.jimdo.com

Website of the Breeding Station `Altes Jagdhaus`:

altes-jagdhaus.jimdo.com

additional Books by Antonia Katharina Tessnow

MADRAS

Magic of the Palm Leafs

The palm leaf library - thousands of years old and an unsolved secret until today. The mystery of this place is the key subject of `Madras`. The true story evolves around one of the greatest secret of mankind.

I have been there. I left my small hometown near Berlin and discovered a legend which says, that every life story is written on a palm leaf; every life story? No, but the live story of all those people, who will undergo the long travel to one of the libraries and search for it. That is what I have done. And this is, what I have found.

People who have read this book:

"A fascinating book. Whoever wants to find the answer to the question: `How many lives do we have?`, will find it here."
Günther Prinz, Managing Director and Chief Editor of 'Bild', Germany.

"So there is my entire life written on a palm leaf in Madras! This book completely changed my understanding of time and space."
Fritz Bloomberg, Ex-Vicepresident Burda Press, New York

"Mind blowing! The ideal book for everybody who wants to learn about the unbelievable truth behind our existence."
Gregor Tessnow, Germany
Author of the bestseller and the script of 'Knallhart'
His novel was filmed in 2006

Astro Calendar

With Ephemerides, Planetary Charts and Moon Phases

Every year new!

The Astro-Calendar is supposed to serve as a way-wiser throughout the year. It doesn't only provide the information needed by an astrologer, but also appeals to everyone who feels a deep connection to nature, to the tides and to the orbiting planets around us. This is why this calendar serves Hobby-Astrologers as well as professionals, whose work depends on the exact sidereal time given by the ephemerides.

In the beginning there is a blank horoscope for you to write your personal chart or any chart you wish. Further the progressions of the planets are graphically represented, also in charts, and this way visually accessible. Before each month the ephemerides for that particular time are listed, so that you always have the entire planetary positions during the entire course of the year right with you. The transitions of the sun and the moon from one sign to the next are also listed right on the corresponding days. May this calendar help all those who want to have the planetary influences, which we are all subjected to, always in sight.

Your feelings of connectedness with the universe will deepen over time and you will develop the most accurate sensitivity and gain a great understanding for the different planetary positions and their energetic influences on us and the entire world.

Madras

Zauber der Palmblätter

Die Palmblattbibliotheken: Tausende Jahre alt und bis heute ein ungelöstes Rätsel. Das Geheimnis dieses Ortes ist das Thema dieses Buches. Die Geschichte dreht sich um eines der größten Rätsel der Menschheit.

Eine Reise führte mich dort hin. Ich habe meine kleine Heimatstadt verlassen um der Sagenumwobenen Legende auf den Grund zu gehen, die besagt, dass dort alle Lebensgeschichten aller Menschen niedergeschrieben sind; allerdings nur von denjenigen, die sich aufmachen, um danach zu suchen.

Eben das habe ich getan. Und dies ist es, was ich gefunden habe.

Dieses Buch liegt in deutscher und englischer Fassung vor.

Menschen, die dieses Buch gelesen haben:

"Ein interessantes Buch. Wer will, findet die Antwort auf die Frage: Wie viele Leben hat ein Mensch?"
Günther Prinz, Publizist, ehemaliger Chefredakteur der 'Bild', Deutschland

"Da steht also mein ganzes Leben auf einem Palmenblatt in Madras. Dieses Buch hat mein Verständnis von Raum und Zeit grundlegend verändert."
Fritz Bloomberg, Ex-Vizepräsident Burda Media, New York

"Ein außergewöhnliches Lesevergnügen, das meine Sicht auf die Welt verändert hat."
Gregor Tessnow, Schriftsteller und Drehbuchautor

Die Botschaft der Tiere

Der Weg zurück zu uns selbst

Ein Wegweiser durch unsere Zeit

Es ist ganz und gar möglich, den Weg nach Hause zu finden. Wir brauchen nicht zu warten, bis wir diese Welt verlassen und zurück in unsere Seelenheimat gehen, um in den ewigen Gefilden Frieden und Liebe zu erleben. Wir können uns unser Zuhause, das Paradies, auch hier auf der Erde, auf diesem Planeten erschaffen. Es ist tatsächlich möglich, uns in ein neues, anderes Bewusstsein hineinzuentwickeln, von dem nicht nur die heiligen Schriften und die Erleuchteten im Laufe unserer Erdgeschichte berichtet haben, sondern von dem uns auch die Tiere erzählen, in dem sie es uns Tag für Tag vorleben.

Wir Menschen können noch umkehren. Wir müssen diese Welt nicht zerstören. Es muss nicht alles so weitergehen wie bisher. Es ist möglich, den Weg zurück ins Paradies zu finden, doch können ihn uns nur diejenigen weisen, die ihn kennen.

Wenn wir den Tieren erlauben, uns den Weg zu weisen, werden wir ihn finden. Wenn wir ihre Botschaft ernstnehmen, sie verinnerlichen und versuchen, sie zu entschlüsseln, werden wir sie verstehen. Die Tiere haben das Paradies nie verlassen. Wer, wenn nicht sie, könnten uns diesen Weg weisen?

Kommunikation mit Tieren

ein Essay

Tierkommunikation ist keine Kunst, die nur wenigen Auserwählten vorbehalten ist, sondern eine Fähigkeit, die in jedem von uns schlummert und uns allen innewohnt. Es ist nichts, was man lernen muss, sondern es ist etwas, woran man sich erinnern kann, wenn man dafür bereit ist. Dieses kleine Büchlein beschreibt in kurzen, aufeinander aufbauenden Abschnitten die Kommunikation mit Tieren. Es soll dabei helfen, sich an seine ursprünglichen Fähigkeiten zu erinnern und sie wieder nutzbar zu machen; es soll ein Wegweiser sein und zeigen, dass jede Begegnung eine Aufgabe für uns bereit hält, für die es immer eine Lösung gibt und an der wir wachsen können. Alles hat einen Sinn und es lohnt sich, darauf zu vertrauen. Selbst wenn wir ihn manchmal nicht gleich verstehen.

Textauszug: 'Jede Kommunikation ist individuell. Jede Verbindung, jedes Karma einmalig. Manchmal sind die Tiere überhaupt erst dafür da, um dem Menschen die gefühlte, intuitive Wahrnehmung und Kommunikation zu erschließen. Es ist ein Gewinn für alle, wenn der Mensch beginnt, eine Verbindung zu seinem Tier und damit zu sich selbst herzustellen, sich seinen Themen und deren Botschaften zu öffnen und von ihnen zu lernen. Wenn du dazu bereit bist, das Tier in seiner Ganzheit zu erkennen und als gleich-wertig zu schätzen, wenn du dich auf dein Ganz-Sein einlässt und dem Tier genauso erlaubst, es selbst zu sein, wie es das Tier dir erlaubt, dann entsteht wahre Verbundenheit. Wenn du über die weit verbreiteten Trainingsmethoden der Dominanz und der autoritären Kontrolle hinauswächst und dich dem tieferen Sinn einer Begegnung zuwendest, wenn du versuchst zu erkennen, was dein Gegenüber dir beibringen will, dann beginnt die Kommunikation mit deinem Tier.

Bolonka Zwetna

*Von der Empfindsamkeit der Hundeseele
und der Liebe, die sie schenkt*

Der Nr. 1 Bestseller in amazon in der Kategorie 'Hunde'

Dieser kleine Ratgeber soll nicht nur zum allgemeinen Verständnis der Beziehungen von Hunden zu uns Menschen beitragen, sondern vor allem den Menschen in seiner Seele berühren. Neben kurzen Überblicken über Rassestandard, Ernährung, Fellpflege und Haltung führt die Autorin den Leser in die facettenreiche Welt der Hundeseele, die voll tiefer Empfindsamkeit ist und niemanden unberührt lässt, der die Fähigkeit besitzt, zu fühlen.

Antonia Katharinas Liebe gilt seit jeher den Tieren. Viele Jahre war sie hauptberuflich in der Reiterei tätig bevor sie Heilpraktik, ganzheitliche Psychologie und Tierheilpraktik studierte. Seitdem widmet sie ihr Leben den Kleinhunderassen im Allgemeinen und dem Bolonka Zwetna im Speziellen. Neben ihrer schriftstellerischen, musischen und tierheilpraktischen Arbeit hat sie sich auf die Auftragsmalerei von Tierfotos spezialisiert und betreut ihre kleine Rassehundezucht der 'Zarenhunde aus dem Alten Jagdhaus'.

Die Hundezucht 'aus dem Alten Jagdhaus'
präsentiert sich unter

rund-um-hunde.jimdo.com

HAIR

Alles über alternative Haarpflege

HAIR - Alles über alternative Haarpflege, ist ein heilpraktisches Sachbuch. Es gibt in den einleitenden Kapiteln einen Überblick über die Inhaltsstoffe in herkömmlichen Shampoos und Duschgels und wie schädlich synthetisch hergestellte Chemikalien in der täglichen Anwendung auf Haut und Haaren sind. Des weiteren wird auf die Langzeitschäden eingegangen, die sich durch den dauerhaften und wiederholten Kontakt mit diesen Chemikalien ergeben können.

Der Hauptteil des Buches zeigt Alternativen zu herkömmlichen Produkten auf, die leicht umzusetzen und anzuwenden sind. Es wird auf komplizierte Anwendungstechniken verzichtet und ganz gezielt die Einfachheit der Methoden betont und in den jeweiligen Anwendungsbeschreibungen dargelegt. Alle alternativen Methoden zur Haut- und Haarreinigung sind von mir persönlich im Selbstversuch getestet, für jeden Interessierten leicht nachvollziehbar und die entsprechenden reinigenden Substanzen leicht erhältlich.
Im letzten Teil des Buches wird auf die Lebensweise, die Ernährung, Öle, Haarbürsten und Tipps und Tricks eingegangen, die langfristig und nachhaltig für gesunde und volle Haare sowie für gesunde, vitale und frische Haut sorgen.

Ziel dieses Buches ist es, das Bewusstsein für den Umgang mit unserem Körper, unserer Umwelt und damit unserer Gesundheit zu schärfen.

Tattoo – Laser – Cover Up

Wenn der Traum zum Albtraum wird

Sowohl das Tätowieren als auch das Lasern ist nicht nur ein Eingriff in deinen Körper, sondern auch in deine Persönlichkeit und dem daran gekoppelten Gefühl, dir selbst gegenüber. Tätowieren verändert einen Menschen; mitunter hat diese Veränderung weitreichende Folgen und hinterlässt tiefe Spuren in deiner Seele. Festzustellen, dass dir das langersehnte Tattoo nicht gefällt oder gar misslungen ist, ist zudem eine schmerzliche Erfahrung, für die es wenig Helfende und Mitfühlende gibt.

Dieses Büchlein soll nicht nur eine Hilfestellung für Betroffene sein, sondern auch die Gedanken derer anregen, die mit der Idee spielen, sich unter die Nadel zu legen. Nicht nur meine eigenen Erfahrungen rund um das Thema Tattoo – Laser – Cover Up sind hier offengelegt, sondern es wurde auch ein Blick in all die Seelenschmerzen und inneren Qualen gewährt, die mit solchen Erfahrungen verbunden sind.

Jede Krise enthält eine Chance, weswegen die Chinesen dafür ein und dasselbe Wort verwenden. Die Chancen dieser Krise sind die daraus entsprungenen, weiterführenden und sehr hilfreichen Gedanken sowie all die wichtigen Überlegungen zum Tätowieren allgemein, die dir hoffentlich helfen mögen und die du unbedingt anstellen solltest, *bevor* du eine Entscheidung triffst, die dich in jedem Fall für dein Leben zeichnen wird.

Breakable - Zerbrechlich

Der Skandalroman aus Mecklenburg

Dieser Psychokrimi hat in der Region, in der es erschien, für so viel Wirbel gesorgt, dass sogar die Presse in die Geschichte eingestiegen ist. Anfeindungen, Intrigen und Klagen finden nicht nur im, sondern fanden auch um das Buch herum statt. Näheres ist einzulesen auf dem Blog

breakablezerbrechlich.wordpress.com

Klappentext:

Eine Frau aus der Stadt. Ein kleines Dorf. Eine alte Köhlerkate, traumhafte Umgebung und idyllische Umgebung. Nicolas Leben könnte nicht friedlicher sein. Eines Tages begegnet sie einem Bauern aus der Nachbarschaft. Es ist Liebe auf den ersten Blick. Als diese von dem Mann mit der unverwechselbaren Stimme auch noch erwidert wird, scheint ihre Welt perfekt.
Doch Nicolas Glück ist nur von kurzer Dauer. Trug und Lüge lauern hinter jeder Ecke. Gerade als sie beginnt, das Ausmaß des Bösen zu entdecken, tun sich Abgründe auf, in die sie niemals hätte schauen dürfen.

Nach einer wahren Begebenheit.

'In ihrem spannenden Roman voller überraschender Volten und psychologischer Abgründe begegnet der Leser Figuren, die er seit Langem zu kennen glaubt.'

Henrik Leschonski, Lektor

Winston

Eine Pferdebuch-Trilogie für Jugendliche

Da Antonia Katharina selbst viele Jahre als Berufsreiterin tätig war, greift sie hier auf einen langjährigen Erfahrungsschatz zurück und veranschaulicht die Welt der Pferde für jeden Leser so realistisch und wirklichkeitsnah, dass man meint, selbst am Geschehen Teil zu nehmen. Ein Pferdeleben, wie es authentischer nicht beschrieben werden kann.

Winston Band I

Ein Fohlen erblickt die Welt

'Da steht er nun. Seine Beine sind viel zu lang für seinen kleinen Körper. Er versucht sich mühsam in der Koordination seiner Bewegungen, die anfangs nur bedingt gelingen. Das Fohlen macht seine ersten Gehversuche und stakst dabei durch das Stroh wie ein Storch durch den Salat.
Es ist wackelig auf den Beinen. Das Neugeborene drückt seinen Körper fest an den seiner Mutter, um stehen zu bleiben und nicht umzukippen. Die Stute bleibt regungslos stehen und wartet, schaut ihr Fohlen an und wagt nicht, sich zu bewegen, sondern bietet mit ihrem großen, ausgewachsenen Körper dem Kleinen Stütze und Orientierung.'

Winston Band II

Die große Show

'Ich wünsche mir aus tiefstem Herzen, dass der Ort, an dem ich bin und alles andere mein Leben lang so bleiben wird wie in diesem Sommer. Das alte Gestüt, in all seiner Stille, entwickelte sich zum unvergesslichen Ort meiner Sehnsucht. Hier will ich sein. Hier gehöre ich her. Und in meinen stillen Augenblicken gibt es nichts, was mir fehlt.
Zwar weiß ich, dass es für die Menschen hier darum geht, Geld zu verdienen, Erfolg zu haben, die Pferde ordentlich auszubilden und teuer zu verkaufen. Doch für mich geht es um den Geruch von frischem Stroh, wenn ich morgens in den Stall komme; um das Glück, das mich durchströmt, wenn ich meine Fohlen auf die Weide lasse; um die Sehnsucht in Winstons Augen, um die warme Sommerluft an lauen Abenden und den unendlichen Frieden, der über den Weiden liegt.
So gingen die Tage ins Land. Alles verlief ruhig. Bis zu jenem Tag, als etwas geschah, was diese Stille durchbrach.'

Winston Band III

Nichts ist unmöglich

'Mein Winston. Niemals hätte ich gedacht, dass man so eine tiefe und innige Beziehung zu einem Pferd haben kann. Dass man sich mit einem Tier so gut verstehen, so klar die Gefühle und Gedanken des anderen erfassen kann; und das alles ohne Worte. Ja, dass man ein Zusammengehörigkeitsgefühl entwickeln kann und eine Nähe, wie das bei uns der Fall ist und das manche Menschen mit allen Worten der Welt niemals herzustellen in der Lage sein werden.'

Copyright of the Original by Antonia Katharina Tessnow

Mecklenburg-Vorpommern, Oktober 2017

ALL RIGHTS RESERVED. No part of this book may be reproduced in any form or by any electronic or mechanical means including information storage and retrieval systems without permission in writing from the publisher, except by reviewers who may quote brief passages in a review.